T0129113

L Y R I C A L
Afrodisiac

L Y R I C A L
Afrodisiac

Erotic Poems & Vignettes

AMERIKAH THE BEAUTIFUL

authorHOUSE®

AuthorHouse™
1663 Liberty Drive
Bloomington, IN 47403
www.authorhouse.com
Phone: 1 (800) 839-8640

Published by AuthorHouse   03/31/2016

ISBN: 978-1-4817-5454-5 (sc)
ISBN: 978-1-4817-5453-8 (e)

Library of Congress Control Number: 2013909334

Print information available on the last page.

Any people depicted in stock imagery provided by Thinkstock are
models, and such images are being used for illustrative purposes
only.
Certain stock imagery © Thinkstock.

This book is printed on acid-free paper.

Lyrical Afrodisiac is dedicated to all those who said I could, I did! Thanks & I love you.

CONTENTS

You Too...

Gasping for air
Madness...

Fingers tangled in my hair
Hysterical...

Dew filled eyes close tightly
High...

Imagine my pelvis touching the sky, legs spread wide
Part my lips sipping my dripping juices, mmmmmm
Closer, luring me in as your face deepens
My ocean covers your bristles exuding
The scent of pleasure surrounds our bodies
Souls glowing showcasing the magnificence of Black love
Melanin tight, fitting him like a glove lost inside love
We travel places unseen, third eye keen
Muffled screams and deep breathing turn into...

I miss you, I miss you too

I love you, I love you too…

Love Lock

Holding me close, the bristles from his beard caress
my neck, and I love it,

Eyes sealed, hearts open wide, as our arms
intertwine the great divide subsides

We find comfort in the ritual of loving from our soul,
controlling the energy around us

Levitating on trust, high...a rush of passion percolates
through our veins,

We remain an archetype of Black love, smeared
stains of pheromones transferred with each touch,

Clairvoyance allows the language of lust to stimulate
the deepest crevice of our intellect,

Deliberately bringing light to the darkest night,
illuminating bright boasting true love rests in the arms
of our tight hugs.

Savage

As your lips kiss my knees

you please me...total elation.

straight to my main vain...your dick is like pure
cocaine taking me hiiiiiiigh

Heart racing as I lay beneath you, looking up into
your intoxicating eyes

I'm blinded by how you grab my thighs, when you
drive deep inside...my moans synthesize

Kitten like cries...purring gently in your ear, all you
can hear is me whispering "don't stop, fuck me baby"

The oratory motivation creates a savage like
persona...A ferocious beast whose appetite is
pleased by a carnal feast...a buffet of tender flesh...
softened by sweat that shimmers our skin

A dimly lit candle flickers across the room mimicking
snapshots photographs that capture our intense
sex faces...my back now faces your chest as you
rest your hands on my waist I bow like a submissive
tigress wanting nothing less than your babies
inside me

Thrusting(pause)

Groans (pause)

As you own the moment...an untamed king, wild and
free as you savagely devour me...soft and gentle
queen I release...cream and my screams evoke
a thunder-like roar as I beg for more your pace
becomes suddenly melodic and deliberate...riding the
rhythm of Minnie Riperton's come inside me, now on
my side looking into your eyes, a pleasure tear slides
down my cheek as we release our love

silent

breathing

baby I love how you love me!

Juice Box

He rocks the boat as his tongue floats in my ocean...
he got my juice box flowin like a broken dam...got me
hissin damn at the top of my lungs as I inch away
from his lips...his licks got my hips jerkin back n forth,
round n round, my thighs rest nicely on his triceps as
his biceps move his forearms into perfect position for
grabbing two portions of my ass...pushing his face
deeper into my treasure giving me pleasure...twirling
my pearl, got this girl ooooo'n and aaaaaah'n, forcin
the back of his head, shifting it into position, keeping
it steady when my body's ready to burst...his thirst for
my cherry keeps him cummin, now I'm creamin down
my thigh... my moans and sighs become silent as I
draw in a deep breath as he looks at me, slithering
slowly up my body applying the pressure of his body
on mine, extending his straw-like tongue between my
lips, sharing sips of the cherry juice box with me.

Symphony 69

The clatter of rain as it hits my window pane serving as the percussion section in our symphonic love session… bodies clashing like cymbals, symbolically stroking each other face-to-face, you brace the back of my neck with the strength of your hands, calculated kisses keep me attentive while your fingers slide back and forth inside me, soft and smooth like piano keys you continue to moisten me, then check to see if I'm ready… by tasting your fingertips as the imaginary timer clicks, you grab my hips swiftly changing my position… I mount your face with jockey-like posture leaning forward like a stealth rider… feeling your hands grip my thighs as your eel-like tongue works its magic causing a waterfall of love juices, cream covers your face like your first birthday cake… my legs continuously shake, then relax as I take you into my mouth, spit drips from my bottom lip adding a hint of wetness to your caramel club starting with the head then inch by inch you vanish… I gag causing your legs to stiffen and feet to point forward. My saliva mixed with semen, some I swallow and the rest slides down your pole which I hold for a few more minutes stroking until all of the stiffness dissipates.

Move me, Groove me

The warm whisper from his lips penetrated my neck and slightly echoed in my ear as he asked if we could dance

I answered with the motion of my hips as they swayed his way and pulled him back in my direction

He gently placed his hands on my waist and allowed me to take him on a ride

Ass firmly pressed against his limp dick I rolled my hips with the force of a small wave gliding back and forth waking up his limpness

My hands were up high reaching for the sky mimicking the movement of a rattlesnake as it entices its prey eyes closely watching, as all self-control was lost became the beams of light that heated our flesh

His hands make their way to mine as we intertwine he takes the lead with his magic stick and I follow like a good little girl who is working for a prize.

Moist from the thrusting of our bodies fighting an ancient battle of the sexes a romance of the ages and a past time that is never forgotten

A marriage and love so intense that no one else in the space exists

But as the song fades out and reality fades in the 5 minute love affair has ended

With our parched throats and limber legs we move apart and give the nod of thanks as we go our separate ways.

He said...

He said my eyes spoke to him

They told him stories of love and passion so deep it made grown men weep

He said my eyes spoke to him

Using vibrant colors of the Sun rays transforming my dreamy chocolate kiss like eyes into a seductive toasted almond shade

He said my eyes spoke to him

Lashes fanning up and down when peeks are exchanged, our reflections dance on the glimmer of our eyes...gazing deeply into each other's soul

He said my eyes spoke to him

Lovely Lip-Service

They assured him that I was his and he was mine...
that time would tell if those eyes he peered into would
ever lose their shine

They are what I first noticed when we met

They are all I can remember when we aren't
face-to-face

They are the first thing I need when we greet

Your face has no meaning without them

They speak volumes, even when they don't utter a sound

As you spew passionate overtures in my ear...your
secret weapons melt me like chocolate...You so gladly
slurp between your soft and chewy...I take them into
mine with the ease and softness they deserve

They are God's gift, created especially for me, they
fit like lock and key when we exchange kisses the
supple flesh becomes a fixture connected by a force
so durable not even the taunts and gestures of the
spectators could pry them apart. This public display
of affection is our way of meeting and greeting,
gives our love a special meaning, and No! We never
have to utter a word because the silence in our lips,
exchange the love that's bellowed between us.

Outside-Haiku

Birds chirping outside
Gently kisses my thigh
Greets morning sunshine

Grass-Haiku

❧

Fresh fluffy and green
Blades of grass tickle my ass
Watching clouds fly by

Fresh-Haiku

Warm breeze passes by
Inhale your seductive scent
You also notice mine… FRESH

Wet-Haiku

❦

Drips juicy liquid
Feels soo good tears slowly fall
Lips softly touch mine

Muddy-Haiku

Cool chocolate brown
Taste yours when it touches mine
Quenching my craving

New Moon-Haiku

Freaks come out at night
New Moon shines bright in the sky
Primal instincts rise

Oh, What A Night!

Driving eagerly patient on a route that is all too familiar, not paying attention to the signs or other cars on the road. Allowing our connection to pull me toward you, my eyes shut and heart opens navigating every curb I turn to get to you.

My pulse intensely getting stronger lets me know my destination is near. As my car eases up to your house and the anticipation of wanting to see you slightly bubbles over in my voice I say in a sweet voice, "I'm outside". The momentary disconnection feels like an eternity until I see the door open. I blink to bring clarity to my vision as I admire all 6ft 2in of your beautiful brown skin. The way your eyes greet my presence lets me know you miss me too.

I step out the car ready to receive your affectionate and loving welcome. I feel you without a single touch, your body heat radiates all around me as you take me into your arms. Your voice low and loving, as you ask me how my day was as if we hadn't spoken all day. Releasing from our loving embrace you grab my hand and lead me into your house and into the bedroom. I soak in all the surroundings, candles dripping specks of light on the lion of Judah blazed with the strength of red, gold, and green.

The heavy base of Beres blazing in the background as we take a seat on the floor to reason about the days happenings. Our legs folded like pretzels seem to create distance between us, so I unfold my legs and intertwine them with yours. Placing my hand on your back, fingertips tracing every word you speak. My smile widens every time you stop our conversation to remind me of my beauty. I can hardly control myself from wanting you every moment I'm in your presence but knowing that the routine of our encounter is what makes it so sweet. I hold my composure.

Jah Cure gracing the play list with his melodic voice when you ask me if I want to dance, we rise from the floor and you grab me close, your chest pressed firmly against my back as our passion fades into the rhythm of you following the lead of my hips rotating round and round, up and down. I turn around to greet your eyes with mine as you lean down to receive my lips. My mouth parts to take yours in, an eternal kiss ends with me slightly biting your bottom lip and slowly letting it go. My eyes are shut enjoying this special moment as you kiss my forehead, my cheek, then softly the nape of my neck, and finally the lotus on my shoulder.

Clothes off, I straddle your back with warm oil in my hands drizzling it in all the peaks and valleys of your masculine structure. Using my hands to smooth it out as I press my fingers in the oil along the tense spots on you back, I can feel you relaxing and taking in the love released from tender touches. I rub my love on you from head to toe and you flip over so that every part of you has received my love. Our kisses become deep and intense as I lift up just enough to take all of you in. Your hands placed intently on my backside as the thrusting movement of our horizontal heaven takes us to another place. Round one coming to an end, we come back to reality and we favor another posture that puts you in control of our lovemaking. Your swelling inside me implies that another round is ending. We both have the stamina for another round but instead decide to conclude our infatuation with tender touches and kisses. Breathing heavy our conversation is minimal as we lay in each other's arms a little while longer.

Our hearts beating hard and fast to the sound of Gyptian as we lay together with our eyes shut. The night is gone and the Sun rises on our moment in time. Feeling like it is the last time every time we see each other but knowing that each day is only a night away from reliving our moment in time. Time and time again. Oh, What a Night!

Thank You,

Sitting on the edge of the bed watching you navigate your way around the room setting the ambiance for a fuck session… full of ecstasy you steal a kiss exhaling the intoxicating scent of purple smoke and candlelight create a strobe light and each flicker shows me all the sexy spots on your body, each tatt perfectly oiled your arms physically strong telling me complete submission is a must… both full of lust Rick Ross and Usher on repeat as you begin at my feet… still looking into my eyes as time flies cuz now your parting my thighs still intently looking into my eyes… your lips gently kiss my inner thigh as I release a sigh, you move in closer to taste my chocolate covered cream pie, the back of my legs resting high on your shoulders making my back arch from the tickle your tongue gave my clit…fuck, shit any expletive will do, as you do your thing Usher sings "Still can't get my mind off your body"… mine jerks as I buss my sixth nut you raise my butt in the air pulling me closer to you, I feel your stiff head moving in a circular motion, entering my warm…wet… thrusting hard and deep making my moans louder with each pump you grab the headboard forcing my back to curl even more as I endure the challenge of pleasing you…I can see the intensity in your eyes… they still haven't lost sight of mine, you slide your hands down to my throat grabbing with enough force to cause painful pleasure…my smaller hands use your wrists as an anchor holding on to a ship in choppy water, I'm leaking all over a mixture of both of our love juices flow as you slowly pull out just enough to flip me over onto my stomach using my scarf as a rope binding my wrists and pulling harder as you plow deeper with each stroke my passionate cries seem to be fueling your stamina…feeling more erect than before, you belt out a as you release, your eyes find mine searching for sign of a job well done…I couldn't help what was to come…cuz that fuck session was full of fun thank you, thank you, thank you oh! Man! Was that fun!

Love Letter

Belly pressed firmly against the springs of my mattress…elbows slightly digging in the creases of the sheets as my fingertips grip my favorite pen…I scribe a letter to the new love of mine…calligraphy paints a portrait of his name between the empty lines filling spaces in my mind…I'm feeling like you could be mine til the end of time but in the mean time we share salty and sweet kisses while watching your Sixers demolish my Knicks, just for kicks we wage a war that leaves us both skin-to-skin, I can tell all bets are off as your hands manipulate my thighs open wide you dive deep inside…as I regain a conscious state, the reality of my dream is an altered state of mind, having you be all mine was just something that crossed my mind and you inspired a few lines…I know this form of communication is obsolete…I just thought it would be sweet if I poured my heart out in the form of ink.

Assibey

Anxiously following the digital voice of my GPS as she guides me to you

my mind flashes back to late night gazes of your delectable double chocolate images

illuminated by the bright light of my BlackBerry

sliding the tip of my thumb across the screen attempting to feel the

essence of your soul locked in the pixels...wanting to paint

you all over me...intently creating a masterpiece that

transcends space and time as we leave beautiful memories

like imprints of butterflies in the moon lit sky...we

fly...or shall I say soar in the future of our past leaving

lasting memories every time we meet...we greet as if we are

past lovers from centuries ago, time never lapses its

continuity is ever-flowing like the Nile...gracefully cool

as the warm breeze sends the scent of you to me...I dip my

hands beneath the liquid love and the refreshing thought of

you caressing me, catapults me back to reality as my

computerized tour guide has ended my ride...my index finger

lightly presses the key that brings your voice to me, gently saying I'm here...your Kingly tone directs me

from point-A to point-B...as you find me...more beautiful than

what was seen in the images that served as duplicates of

me...our conversation is intellectual and playful bouncing

ideas for the next topic off our energy...we retreat

back to the Nile soaking our feet...sipping green tea

talking about loving eternally, imagining what we'll be in

the next century...understanding that today is the first of

many.

Lay

You lay your hands on my waist pulling my hips closer to yours

My foot barely resting on the first step as you snatch my panties below my knees...I silently scream enjoying the feel of you thrusting deeper inside of me, deeper than you've ever been...your left arm resting gently on my neck and hand on my throat applying seductive pleasure

Making me lose my breath as your right hand caresses my breast...the steps seem like the perfect spot as you make a knot in my locks, using them as your anchor delivering spine quivering back shots... aaaaaah.....ssssss

Your index finger becomes my lolly as i ride you high

The stairway in the sky causes thunder between my thighs, creating cloudy skies about the same time I begin to leak a lake that runs down your leg as you prop my ass up on your thigh and release your babies inside me

We lay and breathe

Thinking

We just made a baby.

Collide

When you slide inside…I dream o f creamy days
where I lay in the bliss of you…when you glide past
my thighs with your tongue and your lips play follow
the leader…I become the reader of your inner most
secrets…feelin the freaky mind fuck you moistened
me (drip drip) I'm soakin wet…I can only think about
mounting you for the ride of a lifetime, straddling
your stiff vine as it crawls inside…my voice sends
a cry beyond the blue sky…got heaven and earth
colliding creating an orgasmic explosion of stars
that moisten our bodies with the glow of sex and the
smell of lust…my clit becomes the straw as you suck
me dry and I I I I stutttter as you create a deep arch
in my back with each gulp of me, feeling my energy
deplete…you strategically flip me into a position that
wakes me…face down, ass up as I pull forward on
the tip of your cock and then ease back to engulf all
of you…I become an ocean, wettin you like a water
slide…holdin my hips trying to control how slide on
your pole…your moans excite me even more I switch
gears…ass poppin up and down feeling the muscle
lost in me jump (thump thump) gracefully sliding
the kitty off…you utter oooh baby and my mouth
becomes the warmest place for your release…you
look down at me and pure satisfaction is the image
we see.

Remedy

Its early in the morning and I'm laying in bed having a cup of tea, wondering what you think of me...I know your apprehensive about trusting...your deepest secrets often take you to the darkest places...leaving me behind cuz in your mind the burden is too large for me to bare...concocting ways to keep me at bay far away from loving you through this endless pain... each time I try to provide you with a dosage you hide using time as a wedge to divide you and I...feel your affliction cuz it mirrors mine and that sting we feel deep inside will subside...eventually die, giving way to the bluest of skies allowing us to notice all the sunshine that previously passed us by.

Minds talking during sex pt. 1

He is 6ft tall, cocoa brown, 185 pounds of Charleston chew...lickable honey dew standing nude with his slightly crooked dick inviting me to a show that I must participate in. As he slowly pulls my t-shirt up and over my head my dark almonds are revealed and he instantly releases his twisted tongue onto the barbaric rings that have spliced my nipple in 2...taking a mouth full of my almond joys in with the intensity of a baby yearning for its mothers milk...He is filling me up with his fingers making a small stream leak between my legs and his movement takes him down to my stream as he slurps the juices up not leaving a drop to be wasted. He is staring at me eye-to-eye as he slides his slightly bent pipe in side my warm and wet... taking me on a ride that only he can provide...the fee payable with kisses I give him...gently placing each in the spots only known to me...right behind his ear or tongue kissing the third eye of his crooked pipe is what he likes...so I give him more than usual on these days simply because he is.

Minds talking during sex pt. 2

Jermaine Mind: Now let's really recap on last night I had you all to myself and I didn't want to share for this one moment out of my dreams. You were there I dreamed of this time and finally it became flesh.

Kammy Mind: As your juicy lips embrace my pussy your tongue digs in my clit sending vibrations up my spine...my back arches like a horse shoe as I flip outta my mind...the quakes and shakes your snake gives me...rattles my thighs giving me the ultimate high as I sigh the lovin is so good I begin to cry releasing tears of pleasure...our love making is disguised.

Jermaine Mind: You smile at me, gave me a simple kiss and put my loving to the test I had you and fulfilled all those freaky things at a point I was submissive. I was dominating. We broke a lot of things.

Kammy Mind: The bedroom couldn't hold us, so we started to explore

Making love in the shower, all the way to kitchen floor

Jermaine Mind: Last night I had you and nothing was out of bounds For within these sexual passionate moments, a new animal was found This animal was cunning and she was delighted with squeals She

sunk her teeth into decadence, as if it was her last
meal

Kammy Mind :Last night I had you and the company
we both enjoyed The sun couldn't stop us, as our
playtime indulgence we employed The only thing that
stopped us, is that our cum was overspent So now I
close my eyes, so I can have you all over again

Kammy Baby Let Me Walk You To Your Car Mmm
Your Eyes Jermaine Kammy Your Lips Dam Notice
We Only Spoke When We Departed

Rise

In a slow syncopated motion his chest rises and
falls with the ease of each breath...as he sleeps so
deep...I watch his lids move with the speed of his
dream...his hand motions me to join in, the noise of
the whip cracks against my skin,
drippin wettttt...Black silicon shines, reflecting as
my knees are pressed firmly on the ground, the
tentacles of the whip control my movements and with
each stroke I become an ocean...molasses sliding
down my thighs...you yank the chain around my neck
tighter, stiffening my posture
we're both standing
at attention...paying attention to the softest spots
just below the small of my back, moving into each
position with precision
your fingers slide on my shiny backside like fingers
strumming the heavy baseline we lose track of time...
collecting all my sighs, while deep inside, you ask
whose pussy is this and I quickly reply...baby its
MINE

In the darkness (Shadow)

In the darkness
As we lay with the flickering lights of candles
contouring our bodies
Our eyes meet seeing only the deepest parts of each
other
Recognizing the unrecognizable,
As your moist lips kiss my eyelids shut, I return
the favor, ensuring that we use all of our senses to
innerstand the level of this journey we're on.
The delicious aroma of sex and sweat fill the air
Over-powering the fading strawberry fragrance,
whose only purpose is for lighting the darkest parts of
our bodies.
Rubbing each others most sensual slices as if the
sensation of each others flesh invites us to be a
shadow for one another
Standing, laying, rolling, and searching for a
comfortable place that we could call our own, if only
for a moment.
The intense heat begins to rise and fall with every
breath we take.
The occasional misbeats of our hearts remind us that
we are two instead of one. Two instead of one
I keeping reminding myself that we are one for
only a fraction of a lifetime, but knowing that those
fractions could equal a lifetime. I'll keep enjoying our
occasional shadows.

The Sweetest Thing

When I think of us,

My mind plays the sweetest melody, of warm
summer nights spent in your presence being mentally
stimulated by your essence

As your scent catches a ride on the breeze past my
nose...my eyes close

And I...

Breathe traces of you

It feels like a sin to think of the things my lips could do
once placed on your skin

Subtle nibbles trade places with carnal instinct as you
dig deep

I manage to silently weep "Oooooooo daddy"

Taking a handful of my hair jerking my head toward
the sky so I could look you in the eye, thrusting even
deeper inside as my juices begin to slide down my
thigh...slowly leaving my warm center I feel every
inch exiting...then entering my mouth as you taste
me and I pleasure you...moan louder and louder
as I swallow more and more, nearly performing
a magic trick with your thick stick...disappearing

and reappearing with the speed of light...you fight trying to prolong the inevitable...even though it feels incredible you want five more minutes of my soft luscious lips to keep performing tricks...some things can't be controlled and holding back is a thing of the past as you blast your warm milky cream...I open wide.

Face Down

Face pressed firmly against the pillow as the warmth
of your breath causes tension between my thighs,
your oily hands glide up and down the dotted line
that doubles as my spine…sweet kisses turn into
soft nibbles as you enter my warmth thrusting in and
out using my moans as energy to drive even deeper
inside passionate bites mask the seductive pain of
your teeth sinking into my flesh…you're the conductor
of this carefully orchestrated love session using your
hands to signal changes in position…my back is
arched high…ass kissin the sky prodding me with
your live wire sending electrical currents through me
altering my state of mind…I feel you holding back
as your grunts and groans force you even deeper
inside…you place your hands on my throat and apply
pressure as you plow…creating an ocean that leaks
graciously down my "v" shaped slide…you rest your
chest against that dotted line that doubles as my
spine and whisper are you ready and I reply all the
time.

Sweetest Taboo

You're like the sweetest taboo...warm and pleasing, a delectable treat that tastes oh so good knowing that with every chew I consume you, devouring the toffee that is your lips...taking all of you into the deepest parts of my soul, entering my flesh with such a gentle force that it hurts so good, I cultivate every movement we share like virgin hands reaching for a rose in full bloom...tenderly grasping all of its beautiful agony and not wanting to let go but the stinging pain of our reality reminds me that this tick in time could be our last...the burden of our deceitful love weighs heavily on my heart, trying to maintain balance like lady justice...the constant tug of war between what's right and wrong...between him and you...you and me...you and him...him and me...we are tangled in a web that is too sticky for me to get out of, too sticky to choose. Selfishly thinking I don't want to have to choose. Wanting him just as much as I want you...who says we can't be one big happy family. You loving me, him loving me and me loving the both of you...there is more than enough love to go around in this triad of devotion

Lunch

We had been working hard all week not spending more than 20 waking minutes in the same room and it had finally started to get to us. Looking into his eyes as we said our goodbyes that morning had given me the feeling that he needed my touch to revive him and my eyes were definitely screaming for his touch.

All morning at work I couldn't get the look in my husbands' eyes out of my mind. I asked my secretary to clear my schedule for the rest of the day and decided to pay my husband a visit at work.

It was a good thing that I had worn the tightest skirt-suit to work with no panties and plenty of cleavage. I made a few stops on my way picking up some fruit, whipped cream, and handcuffs.

As I confidently walked down the street concocting what I would do to him…the smile on my face glowing brighter than the sun that day. I finally arrived at 269 Main Street…took the elevator up to the 4th floor and patiently waited for his last client of the day to leave.

Surprised to see me…He asked, "Is everything ok" and I softly responded "yessss". He told the secretary to hold all calls. We walked in the office and shut the door behind us.

"I brought you lunch today babe" as I pulled things from my bag his eyes met with mine as his mouth gently parted he said in a hushed voice "oh I see".

I entered his space as he was sitting partly on his desk and loosened up his tie to take it off. I softly kissed his neck and unbuttoned his shirt. He looked nervous, but couldn't bring himself to stop me. I grabbed his hand and led him to the small couch in the corner of the office; I pushed him down with minimal force and took his shoes off…then his pants. I teased his eyes as I slid my tight skirt off my waist and stepped out of it, took off my jacket and with fruit and whipped cream in hand I slowly fed my husband the appetizer of his lunch. Then I slowly licked his lips, kissed his cheek, going back and forth between licks and kisses until I ended up with his thickness in my mouth. I softly sucked life into his mic singing a song that was juicy and wet hands firmly holding the tool that allowed me to control his breathing from below. He made the music I wanted to hear and let go as I took his protein in to my mouth, I gladly swallowed. With is head resting well on the arm of the couch I moved up so that all he could see was my pussy staring him straight in the eyes. He placed his hands around my midriff with a determination and slid his tongue inside my…and outside my…and all around my walls…causing the nectar to flow between us and create a scent that only love could make. Biting my lips and controlling my volume I enjoyed the mouth that hasn't spoken to me like this all week and mmm it was speaking to me sooo good. I paused the session briefly to go to my bag…taking the cuffs out I helped him up from the couch and sat him in the chair at his desk…cuffed his hands to the chair so he couldn't touch me just enjoy what I had to give.

Giving the mic another tune, I turned my back to him and sat on his lap like I was a little girl telling Santa how good I had been all year. My back arched and legs spread apart…I rode into the sunset like a cowgirl…controlling his breathing that were now pants of ecstasy. Turning around so that I could lick the rest of my juices from his lips… he filled me all the way up as my legs were straddled around his waist as if I were riding for the rodeo championship. There was a fast and hard knock at his door, it excited me, and I rode even faster. His partner was calling his name and I rode even harder. He began swelling even more inside me then I felt his chest rise and fall with mine and we both took a deep breath and let go. Holding him a little longer…then letting go slowly I got up and uncuffed him. He looked more than pleased with our unscheduled lunch date.

I gather my belongings cleaned myself up, kissed him on the lips and left as quickly as I had come. Thinking as I walked back to the train what a wonderful lunch date.

Prey

Today we trade places, I'm the predator and he is
my prey...been thinking all day about how I would
slay him, running it through my mind...day dreaming
and fiendin for a taste of him...instant replaying the
satisfaction on his face...he walks in from a long day
at work he barely even notices the trap I set...the
sensual scene that will unleash the beast in me...he
proceeds to the shower as I slowly slink behind him...
my adrenaline heightening all of my senses...I slide
the shower door open and step in...Close...personal
space nonexistent. He faces me, eyes tired, lips
ready to part and speak, only my left hand covers
his mouth freezing his speech...tongue tracing a
deliberate path down his chest gently kissing his flesh
taking in sips of water, savoring his sweetness...as
the steam from the shower surrounds us increasing
the temperature, I venture towards his shaft...sucking
the tip like my favorite flavor Ring-pop...grabbing
hold with both hands, one beneath the other sliding
them up and down causing titillating friction with his
enormous erection...I devour him deep in my throat...
gagging and pulling him closer I release my hands
from his meat placing them on his waist comfortably
holding him in my mouth his moans feed my ego and
I go harder allowing my throat to be his playground
taking a swig of his pre cum washing away the salty
taste as I admire the pleasure on his face, he braces
as my tongue twisting tricks with the roof of my mouth

and cheeks make him weak, I seek an explosion so I suck even harder knocking hoover outta business he grabs my mahogany locks with extreme force plowing deep... his semen seeps down my throat as he slides out I taste his nature leaving a sample on my lips... tongue moving counter clockwise then biting my bottom lip cuz I defeated him...*Wink.

Divine Stars

I'm really loving this feeling
Enjoying this healing

warming me
Seeing you

Creates smiles, my dimples...wide like sunshine
laughing in the sky

Divine stars fall as I somersault through your mind

Souls harmonized,
In tune with every beat...pulsating simultaneously

Imprinting impermeable tattoos beneath the surface,
carefully stitched to perfection

Chest to chest, warm flesh touching, channeling
energy within

Deeper in, you enter me spiritually
Awakening an Empress loving her King

Nourishing him, breathing life into him

I would gladly dream this dream again, then live it
over and over again and again with HIM.

Breathe

Like exhaling smoke
He spoke to my soul
Filling me to the brim
My heart singing "I truly love him"
He is the ballad of my existence
Standing tall and proud just as a king should
He would give me his last breath and for that he gets
my very best
No need to put him through a silly test
Just cuz other women haven't had this…kind of lovin
has no boundaries
A seamless tapestry perfectly made for you, by me
Made with the purest love
The kind that is only made possible by The Lord up
above
The kind that shakes the earth and leaves the
atmosphere
There is no fear of failure
Your doubts don't exist
This is the realest
Like inhaling smoke
My soul spoke to him
Filling him to the brim

Sexual Insanity

I must be suffering from some abnormality.

It constantly plagues my thinking.

The sweet aroma of a cherry Blow Pop guides my mind to the softness of a red pillow you placed beneath my knees.

While my cherry lips are wrapped around your chocolate covered sucker…Oh my!

poppin and smackin.

Mmm, so thick.

Mmm, so sweet.

As the fruit of you dangles on my bottom lip…I slowly lick.

The tip of my tongue forcing the fantastic flavor of you deep in my throat

Just as I gulp, I'm reminded why we're meeting.

I'm not well.

I had to seek treatment for this major ailment.

I simply can't control it, the flicker of the sunshine peeking through the blinds in your office takes my mind to flashing lights.

Now I'm bent over the hood of your squad car, as you ravage me from behind.

Lifting up my plump cheeks to dig deep.

One, two, three, snaps bring me back to reality.

Calmly sitting across from you in a cozy chair

My eyes document each of your facial expressions

You intently listen as I leak all of my dirty secrets

They peak your interest, which seems to be causing some discomfort

Unable to stay still in your seat, you twist your body as you twist the pearls around your neck

Sweat begins to form on your forehead…there is just no helping me

I came for peace of mind.

Instead, I had a piece of you.

I would give anything just to have sexual sanity.

Suddenly

Your guard fell

Suddenly,

Like the sweat from your forehead disappearing without a trace, allowing the floodgates of love to swoosh my way

I never thought I'd see the day your words would carry me away

Millions of tiny pillows swallow me whole as I nestle in the embrace of your warm words

"I love you baby"

It seems like I've been waiting a lifetime

A super long time, for our hearts to contact our minds and realize each time your lips touch mine

Time stood still and allowed my kisses to perfectly penetrate all the places previously missed...the star I wished on brought you to me and I'm exactly where I wanna be

Here,

With you baby.

My Body is Calling

My body is constantly calling

The feeling takes over me

All I want is to release

So I unleash the beast that hides beneath my bashful personality

Needless to say I've been diagnosed with split personality disorder

And in order to keep them both in order I need an order of hot and steamy

Ready for you bring that thing, make me sing a sweet tune as I cream

Baby be my constant machine,

No hang-ups about pleasing me

You're all I want and need when my body is calling.

Lost & Found

Love was hiding from me in the oddest places

Sent to me hidden behind artificial faces that make false statements Honest lies were the cause of all my cries

Not knowing that in due time God would send me mine

My King who yearns for me to wear his ring on the finger connected to my heart

I didn't have to look hard or even far, I just needed to be patient and baby here you are.

Tickle My Fancy

Different people use me for different reasons, some good and some bad but they still have to stroke me the same. Some stroke me soft and others stroke me hard. Some people aren't that familiar with me so they pay close attention while they stroke me, while others are so in tune with me they know how to stroke me with their eyes closed. I am no good to the world without being stroked it brings out the best in me, I feel invincible, I move stronger, faster… quicker as I am the puppet that has to be guided. For stroking myself couldn't create the wonders of the mind like the puppet master. She places her fingers on me gently and strokes me with such intensity and thoughtfulness that when she takes a break I miss her touch. I want her fingers; I will go so far to say that I need her fingers to glide across me daily…like lock and key we were meant to be…my keyboard and me.

Printed in the United States
By Bookmasters